INVISIBLE STANLEY

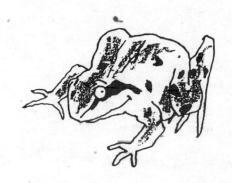

Also by Jeff Brown

Flat Stanley
Stanley and the Magic Lamp
Stanley in Space
Stanley's Christmas Adventure

JEFF BROWN
Author of *Flat Stanley*

INVISIBLE STANLEY

Illustrated by Stephen Lewis

Methuen Children's Books

For
Robert Brown

CB
/JF/C

C 7 069 373 99

First published in Great Britain 1995
by Methuen Children's Books
an imprint of Reed Books Limited
Michelin House, 81 Fulham Road, London SW3 6RB
and Auckland, Melbourne, Singapore and Toronto

Text copyright © 1995 Jeff Brown
Illustrations copyright © 1995 Stephen Lewis

The right of Jeff Brown to be identified as author of this
work has been asserted by him in accordance with
the Copyright, Designs and Patents Act 1988

ISBN 0 416 19122 3

A CIP catalogue record for this book
is available at the British Library

Printed in England by Clays Ltd, St Ives plc

Contents

PROLOGUE

Stanley Lambchop spoke into the darkness above his bed. 'I can't sleep. It's the rain, I think.'

There was no response from the bed across the room.

'I'm hungry too,' Stanley said. 'Are you awake, Arthur?'

'I am now,' said his younger brother. 'You woke me.'

Stanley fetched an apple from the kitchen, and ate it by the bedroom window. The rain had worsened.

'I'm still hungry,' he said.

'Raisins . . . shelf . . .' murmured Arthur, half asleep again.

Crash! came thunder. Lightning flashed.

Stanley found the little box of raisins on a shelf by the window. He ate one.

Crash! Flash!

Stanley ate more raisins.

Crash! Flash!

Arthur yawned. 'Go to bed. You can't be hungry still.'

'I'm not, actually.' Stanley got back into bed. 'But I feel sort of . . . Oh, *different*, I guess.'

He slept.

CHAPTER 1

Where is Stanley?

'Breakfast is ready, George. We must wake the boys,' Mrs Lambchop said to her husband.

Just then Arthur Lambchop called from the bedroom he shared with his brother.

'Hey! Come here! Hey!'

Mr and Mrs Lambchop smiled, recalling another morning that had begun like this. An enormous bulletin board, they had discovered, had fallen on Stanley during the night, leaving him unhurt but no more than half an inch thick. And so he had remained until Arthur blew him round again, weeks later, with a bicycle pump.

'Hey!' a call came again. 'Are you coming? Hey!'

Mrs Lambchop held firm views about good manners and correct speech. 'Hay is for horses, not people, Arthur,' she said as they entered the bedroom. 'As well you know.'

'Excuse me,' said Arthur. 'The thing is, I can *hear* Stanley, but I can't *find* him!'

Mr and Mrs Lambchop looked about the room. A shape was visible beneath the covers of Stanley's bed, and the pillow was squashed down, as if a head rested upon it. But there was no head.

'Why are you staring?' The voice was Stanley's.

Smiling, Mr Lambchop looked under the bed, but saw only a pair of slippers and an old tennis ball. 'Not here,' he said.

Arthur put out a hand, exploring. 'Ouch!' said Stanley's voice. 'You poked my nose!'

Arthur gasped.

Mrs Lambchop stepped forward. 'If I may? . . .' Gently, using both hands, she felt about.

A giggle rose from the bed. 'That *tickles*!'

'Oh, my!' said Mrs Lambchop.

She looked at Mr Lambchop and he at her, as they had during past great surprises. Stanley's flatness had been the first of these. Another had come the evening they discovered a young genie, Prince Haraz, in the bedroom with Stanley and Arthur, who had summoned him accidentally from a lamp.

Mrs Lambchop drew a deep breath. 'We must face facts, George. Stanley is now invisible.'

'You're *right*!' said a startled voice from the bed. 'I can't see my feet! Or my pyjamas!'

'Darndest thing I've ever seen,' said Mr Lambchop. 'Or *not* seen, I should say. Try some other pyjamas, Stanley.'

Stanley got out of bed, and put on different pyjamas, but these too vanished, reappearing when he took them off. It was the same with the shirt and slacks he tried next.

'Gracious!' Mrs Lambchop shook her

head. 'How are we to keep *track* of you, dear?'

'I know!' said Arthur. Untying a small red balloon, a party favour, that floated above his bed, he gave Stanley the string to hold. 'Try this,' he said.

The string vanished, but not the balloon.

'There!' said Mrs Lambchop. 'At least we can tell, approximately, where Stanley is. Now let's all have breakfast. Then, George, we must see what Doctor Dan makes of this.'

CHAPTER 2

Doctor Dan

'What's that red balloon doing here?' said Doctor Dan. 'Well, never mind. Good morning, Mr and Mrs Lambchop. Something about Stanley, my nurse says. He's not been taken flat again?'

'No, no,' said Mrs Lambchop. 'Stanley has remained round.'

'They mostly do,' said Doctor Dan. 'Well, let's have the little fellow in.'

'I am in,' said Stanley, standing directly before him. 'Holding the balloon.'

'Ha, ha, Mr Lambchop!' said Doctor Dan. 'You are an excellent ventriloquist! But I see through your little joke!'

'What you see through,' said Mr
Lambchop, 'is Stanley.'

'Beg pardon?' said Doctor Dan.

'Stanley became invisible during the
night.' Mrs Lambchop explained. 'We are
quite unsettled by it.'

'Head ache?' Doctor Dan asked Stanley's

balloon. 'Throat sore? Stomach upset?'

'I feel fine,' Stanley said.

'I see. Hmmmm . . .' Doctor Dan shook his head. 'Frankly, despite my long years of practice, I've not run into this before. But one of my excellent medical books, *Difficult and Peculiar Cases*, by Doctor Franz Gemeister, may help.'

He took a large book from the shelf behind him and looked into it.

'Ah! "Disappearances," page 134.' He found the page. 'Hmmmm . . . Not much here, I'm afraid. France, 1851: a Madame Poulenc vanished while eating bananas in the rain. Spain, 1923: the Gonzales twins, aged 11, became invisible after eating fruit salad. Lightning had been observed. The most recent case, 1968, is Oombok, an Eskimo chief, last seen eating canned peaches during a blizzard.'

Doctor Dan returned the book to the shelf.

'That's all,' he said. 'Gemeister suspects a connection between bad weather and fruit.'

'It stormed last night,' said Stanley. 'And I ate an apple. Raisins, too.'

'There you are,' said Doctor Dan. 'But we must look at the bright side, Mr and Mrs Lambchop. Stanley seems perfectly healthy, except for the visibility factor. We'll just keep an eye on him.'

'Easier said than done,' said Mr Lambchop. 'Why do his *clothes* also disappear?'

'Not my field, I'm afraid,' said Doctor Dan. 'I suggest a textile specialist.'

'We've kept you long enough, doctor,' Mrs Lambchop said. 'Come, George, Stanley – Where *are* you, Stanley? Ah! Just hold the balloon a bit higher, dear. Goodbye, Doctor Dan.'

By dinner time, Mr and Mrs Lambchop and Arthur had become quite sad. The red balloon, though useful in locating Stanley, kept reminding them of how much they missed his dear face and smile.

But after dinner, Mrs Lambchop, who was artistically talented, replaced the red balloon with a pretty white one and got out her watercolour paints. Using four colours

17

and several delicate brushes, she painted an excellent likeness of Stanley, smiling, on the white balloon.

Everyone became at once more cheerful. Stanley said he felt almost his old self again, especially when he looked in the mirror.

CHAPTER 3

The First Days

The next morning Mrs Lambchop wrote a note to Stanley's teacher, tied a stronger string to his balloon, and sent him off to school.

'Dear Miss Benchley,' the note said. 'Stanley has unexpectedly become invisible. You will find the balloon a useful guide to his presence.

Sincerely, Harriet Lambchop.'

Miss Benchley spoke to the class. 'We must not stare at where we suppose Stanley to be,' she said. 'And not gossip about his state.'

Nevertheless, word soon reached a

newspaper. A reporter visited the school and wrote a story for his paper.

The headline read: 'Smiling Student: "Once You Saw Him, Now You Don't!"' Beneath it were two photographs, a *Before* and an *After*.

The *Before*, taken by Miss Benchley a week earlier, showed a smiling Stanley at his desk. For the *After*, taken by the reporter, Stanley had posed the same way, but only the desk and his smiley-face balloon, bobbing above it, could be seen. The story included a statement by Miss Benchley that

Stanley was in fact at the desk and, to the best of her knowledge, smiling.

Mr and Mrs Lambchop bought several copies of the paper for out-of-town friends. Her colourful balloon artwork lost something in black and white, Mrs Lambchop said, but on the whole it had photographed well.

Arthur said that *Invisible Boy's Brother* would have been an interesting picture, and that Stanley should suggest it if the reporter came round again.

Being invisible offered temptations, Mr and Mrs Lambchop said, but Stanley must resist them. It would be wrong to spy on people, for example, or sneak up to hear what they were saying.

But the next Saturday afternoon, when the Lambchops went to the movies, it was Arthur who could not resist.

'Don't buy a seat for Stanley,' he whispered at the ticket window. 'Just hide his balloon. Who'd know?'

'That would be deceitful, dear,' said Mrs

Lambchop. 'Four seats, please,' she told the ticket lady. 'We want one for our coats, you see.'

'Wasn't *that* deceitful, sort of?' Arthur asked, as they went in.

'Not the same way,' said Mr Lambchop, tucking Stanley's balloon beneath his seat.

Just as the film began, a very tall man sat directly in front of Stanley, blocking his view. Mr Lambchop took Stanley on his lap, from which the screen was easily seen, and the people farther back saw right through him without knowing it. Stanley greatly enjoyed the show.

'See?' said Arthur, as they went out. 'Stanley didn't even *need* a seat.'

'You have a point,' said Mr Lambchop, whose legs had gone to sleep.

CHAPTER 4

In the Park

It was Sunday afternoon. Arthur had gone to visit a friend, so Mr and Mrs Lambchop set out with Stanley for a nearby park. The streets were crowded, and Stanley carried his balloon, to lessen the risk of being jostled by people hurrying by.

Near the park, they met Ralph Jones, an old college friend of Mr Lambchop's.

'Always a treat running into your family, George!' said Mr Jones. 'The older boy was flat once, I recall. You had him rolled up. And once you had a foreign student with you. A prince, yes?'

'What a memory you have!' said Mr Lambchop, remembering that he had

23

introduced as a 'foreign student' the young genie with them at the time.

'How are you, Ralph?' said Mrs Lambchop. 'Stanley? Say hello to Mr Jones.'

'Take care!' said Mr Jones. 'That balloon is floating – Hmmmm .... Just where *is* Stanley?'

'Holding the balloon,' Stanley said. 'I got invisible somehow.'

'Is that so? First flat, now invisible.'

Ralph Jones shook his head. 'Kids! Always one thing or another, eh, George? My oldest needs dental work. Well, I must run! Say hello to that prince, if he's still visiting. Prince Fawzi Mustafa Aslan Mirza Melek Namerd Haraz, as I recall.'

'A truly *remarkable* memory,' said Mrs Lambchop, as Mr Jones walked away.

By a field in the park, the Lambchops found a bench on which to rest.

On the field, children were racing bicycles, round and round. Suddenly, shouts rose. 'Give up, Billy! Billy's no good! Billy, Billy, silly Billy, he can't ride a bike!'

'That must be Billy,' said Mrs Lambchop. 'The little fellow, so far behind the rest. Oh, dear! How he teeters!'

Stanley remembered how nervous he had been when he was learning to ride, and how his father had steadied him. Poor Billy! If only – I'll do it! he thought, and tied his balloon to the bench.

When Billy came round again, Stanley darted on to the field. Taking hold of the teetering bicycle from behind, he began to run.

'Uh-oh!' said little Billy, surprised to be gaining speed.

Stanley ran harder, keeping the bicycle steady. The pedals rose and fell, faster and faster, then faster still.

'Yikes!' cried Billy.

Stanley ran as fast as he could. Soon they passed the boy riding ahead, then another boy, and another! Not until they had passed all the other riders did Stanley, now out of breath, let go.

'Wheeee!' shouted Billy, and went round once more by himself.

'You win, Billy!' shouted the other boys. 'How did you get so good? And so *suddenly*! . . . You sure had us fooled!'

Stanley got his breath back and returned to Mr and Mrs Lambchop on the bench.

'Too bad you missed it, Stanley,' said Mr Lambchop, pretending he had not guessed the truth. 'That teetery little boy, he suddenly rode very well.'

'Oh?' said Stanley, pretending also. 'I wasn't paying attention, I guess.'

Mr Lambchop gave him a little poke in the ribs.

Half an hour passed, and Mrs Lambchop worried that they might sit too long in the sun. In Stanley's present state, she said, over-tanning would be difficult to detect.

Just then a young man and a pretty girl strolled past, hand in hand, and halted in a grove close by.

'That is Phillip, the son of my dear friend, Mrs Hodgson,' Mrs Lambchop said. 'And the girl must be his sweetheart, Lucia. Such a sad story! They are in love, and Phillip wants very much to propose marriage. But he is too shy. He tries and tries, Mrs Hodgson says, but each time his courage fails. And Lucia is too timid to coax the proposal from him.'

Mr Lambchop was not the least bit shy. 'I'll go introduce myself,' he said. 'And pop the question for him.'

'No, George.' Mrs Lambchop shook her head. 'Lucia must hear the words from his own lips.'

An idea came to Stanley.

'Be right back!' he said, and ran to the grove in which the young couple stood. Beside them, he stood very still.

' . . . nice day, Lucia, don't you think?' Phillip was saying. 'Though they say it may rain. Who knows?'

'You are quite right, I'm sure, Phillip,' the girl replied. 'I do value your opinions about the weather.'

'You are kind, very kind.' Phillip trembled a bit. 'Lucia, I want to ask . . . I mean . . . Would you . . . Consent, that is . . .' He gulped. 'What a pretty dress you have!'

'Thank you,' said Lucia. 'I like your necktie. You were saying, Phillip?'

'Ah!' said Phillip. 'Right! Yes! I want . . .' He bit his lip. 'Look! A dark cloud, there in the west! It may rain after all.'

'I hope not.' Lucia seemed close to tears. 'I mean, if it rained . . . Well, we might get wet.'

'This is *very* boring, Stanley thought.

The conversation grew even more boring.

Again and again, Phillip failed to declare his love, chatting instead about the weather, or the look of a tree, or children playing in the park.

'I want to ask, dear Lucia,' Phillip began again, for perhaps the twentieth time, 'if you will . . . That is . . . If you . . . If . . .'

'Yes?' said Lucia, for perhaps the twentieth time. '*What*, Phillip? *What* do you wish to say?'

Stanly leaned forward.

'Lucia . . .?' said Phillip. 'Hmmm . . . Ah! I . . .'

'*Marry me!*' said Stanley, making his voice as much like Phillip's as he could.

Lucia's eyes opened wide. 'I *will*, Phillip!' she cried. 'Of course I will marry you!'

Phillip looked as if he might faint. 'What? Did I – ? You *will?*'

Lucia hugged him, and they kissed.

'I've proposed at last!' cried Phillip. 'I can hardly believe I spoke the words!'

You didn't, Stanley thought.

Mr and Mrs Lambchop had seen the lovers embrace. 'Well done, Stanley!' they

said when he returned to their bench, and several more times on the way home.

Mrs Hodgson called that evening to report that Phillip and Lucia would soon be wed. 'How wonderful!' Mrs Lambchop said. She had glimpsed them in the park just that afternoon. Such a handsome pair! So much in love!

Stanley teased her. 'You said never to sneak up on people, or spy on them. But I did today. Are you mad at me?'

'Oh, very angry,' said Mrs Lambchop, and kissed the top of his head.

CHAPTER 5

The TV Show

Arthur was feeling left out. 'Stanley always gets to have interesting adventures,' he said. 'And that newspaper story was just about *him*. Nobody seems interested in *me*.'

'The best way to draw attention, dear,' said Mrs Lambchop, 'is by one's character. Be kindly. And fair. Cheerfulness is much admired, as is wit.'

'I can't manage all that,' said Arthur.

Mrs Lambchop spoke privately to Stanley. 'Your brother is a bit jealous,' she said.

'When I was flat, Arthur was jealous because people stared at me,' Stanley said.

33

'Now they can't see me at all, and he's jealous again.'

Mrs Lambchop sighed. 'If you can find a way to cheer him, do.'

The very next day an important TV person telephoned Mr Lambchop.

'Teddy Talker here, Lambchop,' he said. 'Host of the enormously popular TV chat show, "Talking With Teddy Talker." Will Stanley appear on it?'

'It would please us to have Stanley *appear* anywhere at all,' Mr Lambchop said. 'People can't see him, you know.'

'I'll just say he's there,' said Teddy Talker. 'Speak to the boy. Let me know.'

Stanly said that he did not particularly care to go on TV. But then he remembered about cheering up Arthur.

'All right,' he said. 'But Arthur too. He likes to tell jokes and do magic tricks. Say we'll *both* be on the show.'

Arthur was very pleased, and that evening the brothers planned what they would do. The next morning, Mr Lambchop told Teddy Talker.

'Excellent plan!' said the TV man. 'This Friday, yes? Thank you, Lambchop!'

'Welcome, everybody!' said Teddy Talker that Friday evening, from the stage of his TV theatre. 'Wonderful guests tonight! Including an invisible boy!'

In the front row, applauding with the rest of the audience, Mr and Mrs Lambchop thought of Stanley and Arthur, waiting now in a dressing-room backstage. How excited they must be!

The other guests were already seated on

the sofa by Teddy Talker's desk. He chatted first with a lady who had written a book about sausage, then with a tennis champion who had become a rabbi, then with a very pretty young woman who had won a beauty contest, but planned now to devote herself to the cause of world peace.

At last came the announcement that began the Lambchop plan.

'Invisible Stanley has been delayed, but will be here shortly,' Teddy Talker told the audience. 'Meanwhile, we are fortunate in having with us his very talented brother!'

Protests rose. 'Brother? A *visible* brother? . . . Drat! . . . Good thing we got in free!'

'Ladies and gentlemen!' said Teddy Talker. 'Mirth and Magic with Arthur Lambchop!'

Arthur stepped out on to the stage, wearing a smart black magician's cape Mrs Lambchop had made for him, and carrying a small box, which he placed on Teddy Talker's desk.

'Hello, everybody!' he said. 'The box is for later. Now let's have fun! Heard the story about the three holes in the ground?'

He waited, smiling. 'Well, well, well!'

Two people laughed, but that was all.

'I don't understand,' said a lady sitting behind Mr and Mrs Lambchop.

Mr Lambchop turned in his seat. 'A "well" is a hole in the ground,' he said. '"Well, well, well." Three holes.'

'Ah! I see!' said the lady.

'A riddle, ladies and gentlemen!' cried Arthur. 'Where do kings keep their armies?'

'Where?' someone called.

'In their sleevies!' said Arthur.

Many people laughed now, including the lady who had missed the first joke. 'I *got* that one,' she said.

'And now a mind-reading trick!' Arthur announced. He shuffled a deck of cards, and let Teddy Talker draw one.

'Don't let me see it!' he said. 'But look at it! Picture it in your mind! I will concentrate, using my magic powers!' Arthur closed his eyes. 'Hmmm . . . hmmm . . . Your card, sir, is the four of hearts!'

'It is!' cried Teddy Talker. 'It *is* the four of hearts!'

Voices rose again. 'Incredible! . . . He can read minds? So young, too? . . . Do that one again, lad!'

'Certainly!' said Arthur.

But he had used a false deck in which *every* card was the four of hearts, and the audience would surely guess if that card were named again. Fortunately, the brothers had thought of this. Backstage, Stanley tied his balloon to a chair.

Arthur now shuffled a real deck of cards,

then called for a volunteer. When an elderly gentleman came on to the stage, Stanley tiptoed out to stand behind him. The audience applauded the volunteer. How peculiar this is! Stanley thought. Hundreds of people looking, but no one can see me!

'Draw a card, sir!' said Arthur. 'Thank you! Keep it hidden! But picture it in your mind!' Again closing his eyes, he pretended to be thinking hard.

A quick peek told Stanley that the

volunteer held the ten of clubs. Tiptoeing over, he whispered in his brother's ear.

Arthur opened his eyes. 'I have it. The card is – The ten of clubs!'

'Yes! Bravo!' cried the old gentleman. The audience clapped hard as he returned to his seat.

Mr Lambchop smiled at the lady behind him. 'Our son,' he said.

'So clever!' said the lady. 'What *will* he do next?'

Mrs Lambchop drew a deep breath. That morning, Stanley and Arthur had borrowed a pet frog from the boy next door. What came next, she knew, would be the most daring part of the evening's plan!

'Ladies and gentlemen!' said Arthur. 'A new kind of magic! Arthur Lambchop – that's me! – and Henry, the Air-Dancing Frog!'

He lifted Henry from the box on Teddy Talker's desk, and held him up. Henry, who appeared to be smiling, wore a little white shirt with an 'H' on it, made by Mrs Lambchop along with Arthur's cape.

41

'Fly, Henry!' cried Arthur. 'Fly out, and stand still in the air!'

Stepping forward, Stanley took Henry from Arthur's hands and ran to the far side of the stage. Here he stopped, holding the frog high above his head. Henry wriggled his legs.

'Amazing!' shouted the audience. 'Who'd believe it? . . . That's some frog! . . . What keeps him up there?'

'Circle, Henry!' Arthur commanded. 'Circle in the air!'

Stanley walked rapidly in circles, swaying Henry as he went.

The audience was tremendously impressed. 'What a fine magician! . . . Mind reading *and* frog flying! . . . You don't see that every day!'

Pretending to control Henry's flight, Arthur kept a finger pointed as Stanley swooped the frog all about the stage. 'Whoops!' cried Teddy Talker as Henry flew above his desk. On the long sofa, the sausage writer and tennis rabbi and the beauty contest winner ducked down.

Even Mr and Mrs Lambchop, knowing
the secret of Henry's flight, thought it an
amazing sight.

At last, to great applause, Arthur took
Henry into his own hands and returned
him to the little box.

Stanley tiptoed off to get his smiley-face balloon. The plan now called for Teddy Talker to announce the arrival of the invisible boy, and introduce him.

But Arthur had stepped forward again.

'Thank you for cheering me,' he told the audience. 'But I have to say something. That first mind-reading trick, I really did do that one. But the second trick – Actually, I can't read minds at all. And the flying frog, he – '

Voices rose. 'Can't read minds? . . . We've been lied to! . . . The *frog* was lying? . . . Not the frog, stupid! Wait, he's not done!'

'Please! Listen!' said Arthur. 'It wouldn't be fair to let you think I did everything by myself. I had a helper! The second trick, he saw the card and told me what it was. And Henry . . . Well, my helper was whooshing him in the air!'

By now the audience was terribly confused. 'Who? . . . What helper? . . . It was just a regular frog? . . . But *some* frogs fly! . . . No, squirrels, not frogs! *Whooshing?*'

Arthur went on. 'My brother Stanley helped me! He fixed it for me to be on this show! He's a really nice brother, and I thank him a lot!'

Teddy Talker had sprung to his feet. 'Ladies and gentlemen! May I present now a very special guest, who has been here all along! The invisible boy! Stanley Lambchop!'

Stanley came on to the stage, carrying his smiley-face balloon. Arthur put out his hand, and the audience could tell that Stanley had taken it. There was tremendous applause.

The brothers bowed again and again, Stanley's balloon bobbing up and down. Arthur's smile was plain to see, and Mr and Mrs Lambchop, as they applauded, thought that even the balloon's painted smile seemed brighter than before.

'I have two children myself,' said the lady behind them. 'Both entirely visible, and without theatrical flair. We are a very *usual* family.'

'As we are,' said Mr Lambchop,

smiling. 'Mostly, that is.'

Arthur left the stage, and Stanley sat on the sofa between the sausage writer and the beauty contest winner and answered Teddy Talker's questions. He had no idea *how* he became invisible, he said, and it wasn't actually a great treat being that way, since he often got bumped into, and had to keep reminding people he was there. After that, Teddy Talker thanked everyone for coming, and the show was over.

Back home, Arthur felt the evening had gone well.

'I got lots of applause,' he said. 'But maybe it was mostly because of what Stanley did. I shouldn't be too proud, I guess.'

'Poise and good humour contribute greatly to a performer's success,' said Mrs Lambchop. 'You did well on both those counts. Return Henry in the morning, dear. Time now for bed.'

CHAPTER 6

The Bank Robbers

Mr Lambchop and Stanley and Arthur were watching the evening news on TV.

' . . . more dreadful scandal and violence tomorrow,' said the newscaster, ending a report on national affairs. 'Here in our fair city, another bank was robbed today, the third this month. The unusual robbers – '

'Enough of crime!' Bustling in, Mrs Lambchop switched off the TV. 'Come to dinner!'

Stanley supposed he would never know how the robbers were unusual. But the next afternoon, while strolling with Mr

Lambchop, he found out. On the way home they passed a bank.

'I must cash a cheque, but it is very crowded in there,' said Mr Lambchop. 'Wait here, Stanley.'

Stanley waited.

Suddenly cries rose from within the bank. 'Lady bank robbers! Just like they said on TV! . . . I laughed when I heard it! . . . Me too!'

Two women in dresses and fancy hats, one stout and the other very tall, ran out of the bank, each with a moneybag in one hand and a pistol in the other.

'Stay in there!' the stout woman called back into the bank, her voice high and scratchy. 'Don't anyone run out! Or else . . . Bang! Bang!'

'Right!' shouted the tall woman, also in an odd, high voice. 'Just because we are females doesn't mean we can't shoot!'

Being invisible won't protect me if bullets go flying about! Stanley thought. He looked for a place to hide.

An empty Yum-Yum Ice-Cream van was parked close by, and he jumped into it. His balloon still floated outside the van, its string caught in the door, but he did not dare to rescue it. Scrunching down behind cardboard barrels marked 'Yum Chocolate', 'Strawberry Yum', and 'Yum Crunch', he peeked out.

An alarm was ringing inside the bank, and now shouts rose again. 'Ha! Now you're in trouble! The police will come! Put that money back where you found it, ladies!'

Then Stanley saw that the two robber women were running towards him, carrying their money bags. They were stopping! They were getting into the Yum-Yum van!

Scrunching down again, he held his breath.

The robbers were in the van now, close by where he hid. 'Hurry up!' said the stout woman, in a surprisingly deep voice. 'These shoes are killing me!'

The tall woman opened the 'Yum Crunch' barrel, and Stanley saw that it was empty. Then both robbers poured packets of money from their bags into the barrel, and put the lid back on again.

Stanley could hardly believe what he saw next!

The robbers threw aside their fancy hats, and tugged off wigs! And now they were undressing, pulling their dresses over their heads!

They were *men*, Stanley realized, not women! Yes! Underneath the dresses they wore white ice-cream-man pants, with the legs rolled up, and white Yum-Yum shirts!

'Whew! What a relief, Howard!' The stout robber kicked off his women's shoes, and put on white sneakers.

'They'll never catch us now, Ralph!' said

the tall one.

The robbers unrolled their trouser legs and threw their female clothing into another empty barrel, the one marked 'Yum Chocolate'. Then they jumped into the front seats, the tall man driving, and the van sped off.

Behind the barrels, Stanley held his breath again. This pair was too clever to be caught! They were sure to get away! No one would suspect two Yum-Yum men of being lady – But the van was slowing! It was stopping!

Stanley peeked out again.

A police car blocked the road, and two policemen stood beside it, inspecting cars as they passed by. In a moment, they were at the Yum-Yum van.

'A bank got robbed,' the first policeman told the driver. 'By two women. You ice-cream fellows seen any suspicious looking females?'

'My!' The tall man shook his head. 'More and more these days, women filling roles once played by men. Bless 'em, I say!'

51

Beside him, the stout man said hastily, 'But bank robbing, Howard, that's *wrong*.'

The second policeman looked into the back of the van. 'Just ice-cream here,' he told his partner.

The trickery is working! Stanley thought. How can I – An idea came to him. Reaching out, he flipped the lid off the 'Yum Chocolate' barrel.

'Loose lid,' said the second policeman. 'Better tighten – Hey! This barrel is full of female clothes!'

'Oh!' The tall robber made a sad face. 'For the needy.' he said. 'They were my late mother's.'

Stanley flipped the lid off the 'Yum Crunch' barrel, and the packets of money were plain to see!

'Your mother was a mighty rich woman!' shouted the first policeman, drawing his pistol. 'Hands up, you two!'

As the robbers were being handcuffed, another police car drove up. Mr Lambchop jumped out of it.

'That balloon, on that van!' he shouted. 'We've been following it! Stanley? . . . Are you in there?'

'Yes!' Stanley called back. 'I'm fine. The bank robbers are caught! They weren't ladies at all, just dressed that way!'

The handcuffed robbers were dreadfully confused. 'Who's yelling in our van? . . . Who stuck a balloon in the door? . . . Have we gone crazy?' they said.

'It's my son Stanley,' said Mr Lambchop. 'He is invisible, unfortunately. Thank goodness he was not hurt!'

'That must be the same invisible boy they had on TV!' said the first policeman.

'An invisible boy?' The tall robber groaned. 'After all my careful planning!'

The stout robber shrugged. 'You can't think of *everything*, Howard. Don't blame yourself.'

The robbers were driven off to jail, and Stanley went home with Mr Lambchop in a cab.

Stanley had been *far* too brave, Mrs Lambchop said when she heard what he had done. Really! Flipping those ice-cream lids! Arthur said he'd have flipped them too, if he'd thought of it.

CHAPTER 7

Arthur's Storm

Mr and Mrs Lambchop had said goodnight. For a moment the brothers lay silent in their beds.

Then Arthur yawned. 'Goodnight, Stanley. Pleasant dreams.'

'Pleasant dreams? Hah!'

'Hah?'

'Those robbers today, they had *guns*!' said Stanley. 'I could have got shot by accident, and nobody would even know.'

'I never thought of that.' Arthur sat up. 'Are you mad at me?'

'I guess not. But . . .' Stanley sighed. 'The

thing is, I don't want to go on being invisible. I was really scared today, and I hate carrying that balloon, but when I don't people bump into me. And I can't see myself in the mirror, so I don't even remember how I look! It's like when I was flat. It was all right for a while, but then people laughed at me.'

'That's why I blew you round again,' Arthur said proudly. 'Everyone said how smart I was.'

'If you're so smart, get me out of *this* fix!' There was a little tremble in Stanley's voice.

Arthur went to sit on the edge of his brother's bed. Feeling for a foot beneath the covers, he patted it. 'I'm really sorry for you,' he said. 'I wish – '

There was a knock at the door, and Mr and Mrs Lambchop came in. 'Talking, you two? You ought to be asleep,' they said.

Arthur explained about Stanley's unhappiness.

'There's more,' Stanley said. 'Twice my friends had parties, and didn't invite me. They forget me sometimes even if I *do* keep waving that balloon!'

'Poor dear!' Mrs Lambchop said. '"Out of sight, out of mind," as the saying goes.' She went to put her arms around Stanley, but he had just sat up in bed, and she missed him. She found him and gave him a hug.

'This is awful!' Arthur said. 'We have to *do* something!'

Mr Lambchop shook his head. 'Doctor Dan knew of no cure for Stanley's condition. And little about its cause, except for a possible connection between bad weather and fruit.'

'Then I'll always be like this.' Stanley's voice trembled again. 'I'll get older and bigger, but no one will ever see.'

Arthur was thinking. 'Stanley did eat fruit. And there *was* a storm. Maybe – Wait!'

He explained his idea.

Mr and Mrs Lambchop looked at each other, then at where they supposed Stanley to be, and at each other again.

'I'm not afraid,' said Stanley. 'Let's *try*!'

Mr Lambchop nodded. 'I see no harm in it.'

'Nor I,' said Mrs Lambchop. 'Very well, Arthur! Let us gather what your plan requires!'

'Everyone ready?' said Arthur. 'It has to be just the way it was the night Stanley got invisible.'

'I'm wearing the same blue-and-white stripey pyjamas,' said Stanley. 'And I have an apple. And a box of raisins.'

'We can't make a real storm,' Arthur said. 'But maybe this will work.'

He stepped into the bathroom and ran the

water in the basin and shower. 'There's rain,' he said, returning. 'I'll be wind.'

Mrs Lambchop held up a wooden spoon and a large frying-pan from her kitchen. 'Thunder ready,' she said.

Mr Lambchop showed the powerful torch he had fetched from his tool kit. 'Lightning ready.'

Stanley raised his apple. 'Now?'

'Go stand by the window,' said Arthur. 'Now let me think. Hmmm . . . It was dark.' He put out the light. 'Go on, eat. *Whooosh!*' he added, being wind.

Stanley began to eat the apple.

Water pattered down in the bathroom, into the basin and from the shower into the bathtub.

'*Whooosh . . . whooosh!*' said Arthur, and Mrs Lambchop struck her frying-pan with the wooden spoon. The *crash!* was much like thunder.

'Lightning, please,' Arthur said.

Mr Lambchop aimed his torch and flicked it on and off while Stanley finished the apple.

'Now the raisins,' said Arthur. 'One at a time. *Whooosh!*'

Stanley opened the little box and ate a raisin.

Still *whooshing*, Arthur conducted as if an orchestra sat before him. His left hand signalled Mrs Lambchop to strike the frying pan, the right one Mr Lambchop to flash the light. Nods told Stanley when to eat a raisin.

Patter . . . splash . . . went the water in the bathroom. *Whooosh!* went Arthur. *Crash!* went the frying-pan. *Flash! . . . flash!* went the light.

'If anyone should see us now,' Mrs Lambchop said softly, 'I should be hard put to explain.'

Stanley looked down at himself. 'It's no use,' he said. 'I'm still invisible.'

'Twist around!' said Arthur. 'Maybe the noise and light have to hit you just a certain way!'

Twisting, Stanley ate three more raisins. The light flickered over him. He heard the water splashing, Arthur *whooshing*, the pounding of the frying-pan by the spoon. How hard they were trying, he thought. How much he loved them all!

But he was still invisible.

'There's only one raisin left,' he said. 'It's no use.'

'Poor Stanley!' cried Mrs Lambchop.

Arthur could not bear the thought of never seeing his brother again. 'Do the last raisin, Stanley,' he said. 'Do it!'

Stanley ate the raisin, and did one more twist. Mrs Lambchop tapped her frying-pan and Mr Lambchop flashed his light. Arthur gave a last *whooosh*!

Nothing happened.

'At least I'm not hungry,' Stanley said bravely. 'But – ' He put a hand to his cheek. 'I feel . . . Sort of tingly.'

'Stanley!' said Mr Lambchop. 'Are you touching your cheek? I see your hand, I think!'

'And your pyjamas!' shouted Arthur, switching on the light.

A sort of outline of Stanley Lambchop, with hazy stripes running up and down it,

had appeared by the window. Through the stripes, they could see the house next door.

Suddenly, the outline filled in. There stood Stanley in his striped pyjamas, just as they remembered him!

'I can see my feet!' Stanley shouted. 'It's *me*!'

'"*I*," dear, not "me!",' said Mrs Lambchop before she could catch herself, then ran to hold him tight.

Mr Lambchop shook hands with Arthur, and then they all went into the bathroom to watch Stanley look at himself in the mirror.

It hadn't mattered when he was invisible, Mrs Lambchop said, but he was greatly in need of a haircut now.

She made hot chocolate to celebrate the occasion, and Arthur's cleverness was acknowledged by all.

'But false storms cannot be relied upon,' Mr Lambchop said. 'We must think twice before eating fruit during bad weather. Especially by a window.'

Then the brothers were tucked into bed again. 'Goodnight,' said Mr and Mrs Lambchop, putting out the light.

'Goodnight,' said Stanley and Arthur.

Stanley got up and went to have another look in the bathroom mirror. 'Thank you, Arthur,' he said, returning. 'You saved me from being flat, and now you've saved me again.'

'Oh, well . . .' Arthur yawned. 'Stanley? Try to stay, you know, *regular* for a while.'

'I will,' said Stanley.

Soon they were both asleep.

The End